FINN & BOTTS

CURSE OF THE CORNFIELD GHOST

FINN & BOTTS

CURSE OF THE CORNFIELD GHOST

STEW KNIGHT

Dreamwell Press

Copyright © 2019 Stewart Knight

Published by Dreamwell Press, Salt Lake City
www.finnandbotts.com

Edited and designed by Girl Friday Productions
www.girlfridayproductions.com

Editorial: Clete Smith, Amy Sullivan, Amy Snyder
Design: Paul Barrett
Illustrations: Mark Meyers

ISBN (Paperback): 978-1-7336092-0-3

First edition

Printed in the United States of America

For Sam

CHAPTER ONE

Finn Fasser always stayed away from the cornfield on his street—especially on Halloween. But on this Halloween, that would change.

"Heeeelp, Finn!"

Finn had no problem recognizing that voice. It was Botts, Finn's best friend.

Finn lived in a neighborhood that once was a large farm with cornfields that went for miles in every direction. Over time, portions of the land were sold to build new streets and homes. The last remaining cornfield was located on Finn's street.

"Over here!" Botts yelled again.

Finn was with Tess walking down Finn's street when the yelling started. Tess was one of Finn's school friends. They had both stayed after school to finish a makeup math quiz. He and Tess ran toward Botts, who was in the middle of the baseball diamond that had been built next to the cornfield. Botts was frantically motioning to them to come over.

"It must be something important," Finn gasped, trying to catch his breath. "You only yell when you're hungry. What's up?"

Botts looked panicked.

"I lost my grandpa's baseball thanks to Taz here," Botts began. Taz was a new student at Penn Wallow Elementary. He and Taz were two of the biggest students at school and had become good friends.

"He hit it right over third base and into there—somewhere," Botts said and pointed to

2

the cornfield. "If we split up, I think we can find it. Taz and I will cover everything left of third base. You and Tess cover everything to the right. Sound like a plan?"

Tess cautiously looked over at the cornstalks. They were tightly packed together in rows that seemed to go on forever. "You could get lost in there," she said, voice trembling. Tess walked over to the first row. Botts and Taz followed. They bent the stalks sideways in search of Botts's baseball. Taz turned back to look at Finn standing and watching. Finn knew his face must have looked as tense as he felt.

"What's the problem?" asked Taz.

"What's the problem?" Finn responded in disbelief. "Tomorrow is Halloween!"

"And why is that a problem?" Taz asked.

"The Cornfield Ghost is in there!" said Finn. "And he's getting ready for his next victim!"

"The Cornfield Ghost?" Taz scoffed.

"Yes!" Finn exclaimed. "Go ahead—laugh it up! Lulu never found her dog after it went into the cornfield to get a ball last Halloween. Or how about the time when Jinx's kite crashed inside the field—exactly a year ago tomorrow? When Jinx got to the end of the string, it was wrapped around an old cornstalk. And the kite was gone. Botts, you remember!"

"Maybe the dog ran away and the kite blew away," Botts suggested. "But let's not worry about it right now. I've got to find the baseball. My grandpa caught it at a World Series game. I can't lose it, or I'm dead."

Finn stuck out his hand as a stop sign. "You'll be dead if you go in there!" he shouted. "And anybody else who tries. The cornfield is cursed. Don't you remember what happens here? Every Halloween, the ghost of old Grim roams this place."

"And just who is this Grim?" Taz smirked.

5

"Grim farmed this land over a hundred years ago," Finn explained. "On Halloween night, some thieves broke into his house and robbed him at gunpoint. They thought they could lose Grim by running into his cornfield—*this* cornfield." Finn pointed toward the field, his face serious as he tried to hide any sign of fear he felt inside. "But Grim grabbed a gun and chased after them. Grim's farmhand tried to help but was too late. A gun went off, and the bell on the well rang out. When the farmhand arrived, the only thing he found was Grim's gun on the ground. The thieves were never caught."

"What happened to Grim?" Tess asked.

"Grim was never found," Finn replied. "Most say he was killed and then pushed into the well. But nobody could ever find the body. Strange things have happened each Halloween since then. Some claim they've heard the bell ringing on Halloween night."

"I remember Jinx telling me he saw an old man in the cornfield," Tess added.

"I bet the ghost of Grim will never go away until he finds the thieves," Finn insisted.

At that moment, two hideous monsters jumped out from behind the cornstalks. Their loud moans mixed with shrieks filled the air. Finn and Tess jumped backward, falling to the ground. Finn clawed the grass with his right hand, desperately trying to pull himself away from the approaching creatures.

"Got you two good," Botts chuckled.

The monsters pulled off their masks. It was Manny and Danny McKinnsey. They were twins. Both of them were in Finn's class at school.

"They didn't see that one coming, did they?" Manny laughed.

Even Tess managed a smile as she got up. "Botts, that was your best prank yet," she added.

Everyone was laughing except Finn. "This is serious," he said. "Two years ago, Teeter ran through the cornfield on Halloween night as a shortcut to get home. He heard someone following him through the field. He ran and hid in some bushes near the old Grim house the entire night. Teeter swore he saw a shadowy figure following him."

"You know Teeter," Botts added. "He gets scared just walking to school."

"You don't have to believe me," Finn grumbled. "Go ahead. Walk right into the field. I hope you're ready. Ready for the police to come looking for you when you go missing."

Finn grabbed his schoolbag, turned, and headed home. He would do everything he could to stay away from the cornfield tomorrow night. This Halloween might be his last if he wasn't careful.

CHAPTER TWO

Finn woke the next morning more tired than when he'd gone to bed. He had spent most of the night dreaming about the Cornfield Ghost chasing him. Suddenly his sister, Selina, burst into his bedroom, slamming the door against the wall.

"Hurry!" Selina yelled. "We need to go now, or you'll be walking to school."

Ms. Twitchel was expecting his help this morning with the Halloween carnival. Finn couldn't be late. He got dressed, ran downstairs, and went into the garage. An old-man mask and straw hat were inside a dusty box on the floor. He grabbed them and raced back to the kitchen. He sat down at the table, slid his schoolbooks into his backpack, and stuffed a warm pancake into his mouth, which Ms. Fasser had just brought over to him on a plate. Selina was standing near the kitchen door, combing her hair. In a bag near Selina's feet, Finn could see a ballet tutu and a set of plastic fangs.

"You're really going to wear your goofy Grim costume again?" Selina asked, snickering. "I can't believe Botts is letting you sit on his shoulders for the second year in a row. Do you really want to parade around as an imaginary dorky tall dead guy?"

"The ghost of Grim is real," Finn replied while trying not to let the last part of his uneaten pancake fall out of his mouth. "You've heard the stories about what happened in the cornfield last October. Besides, how real is a vampire ballerina?"

"Listen, you two," Ms. Fasser interrupted. "The most important thing is for both of you to be safe—especially tonight."

Finn looked over at his mom. "I'm not certain we'll be safe," he said. "Remember last Halloween? Someone in a black cape stole a lot of trick-or-treat bags from some kids in the neighborhood. And we still don't know who it was."

"Maybe you can come up with a plan so that won't happen again," Finn's mom said, smiling. "But for now, let's get both of you to school on time. I'll be in the car."

Finn put his costume into his backpack with his books and followed Selina out the front door. Three minutes later they arrived at school. Both he and Selina jumped out of the car and waved goodbye.

Finn immediately noticed Felix. Felix was dressed as a magician with a long black cape, a tall black hat, and a fake mustache. He imagined Felix walking up to the kids in his neighborhood and telling them he could make their trick-or-treat bags disappear—and then running off with them. It was just the kind of trick Felix would do. *Maybe Felix was the one who stole the bags last year,* he thought. He decided to watch Felix closely today.

When he entered Ms. Twitchel's classroom, it was in total chaos. Lulu, wearing a fairy costume, was waving her wand at Oscar and chanting a magical spell, while Oscar, in his pirate coat and hat, was trying to knock the wand out of her hand with his sword. Veronica, dressed as a princess, was chasing Victor, in a mummy costume, trying to unwind his wrappings. And Taz, wearing a mad-scientist lab coat and rubber gloves, was yelling about the

bubbling liquid oozing out of the beaker he was holding.

Finn looked over at Teeter standing still in the back, covered in a big white sheet with holes cut out for his eyes. This was the same ghost costume Teeter had worn every year for as long as Finn could remember. Teeter was the only person Finn knew who could scare himself.

Finn weaved through the crowd toward the boxes of apples and donuts near Ms. Twitchel's desk. Tess, dressed as a cowgirl, was walking out of the classroom door, carrying two boxes of apples.

"These boxes go down to the cafeteria for today's carnival," Ms. Twitchel said, her big witch hat tilted to one side. "Please hurry, Finn—the parade starts in ten minutes."

Finn put the hat and mask down on his desk, grabbed the two remaining boxes of donuts, and followed Tess down the hallway. The sounds of laughing and a dog barking were coming from a classroom just ahead on the left. It was Bellow's classroom. Bellow was one of the school bullies. It seemed like he was always bothering or teasing someone.

Finn walked slowly over to the doorway, stopped, turned, and then peeked inside. Bellow was up to his usual jokes. He had taken a frog from the glass tank on the back table and placed it on Jenna's desk.

At the rear of the classroom was Sylvia, who lived on the same street as Finn. She was tossing dog biscuits to Seeker, her black poodle. Pets were normally not allowed at school, but the principal had made an exception for the Halloween parade. Seeker was dressed like a clown, and Sylvia was dressed like a circus ringmaster. Finn leaned farther into the doorway and watched with amusement. Seeker walked on his hind legs, rolled over, and then sat perfectly still in anticipation of eating another biscuit.

Sylvia noticed Finn peering into the classroom. Instantly, she instructed Seeker to hold up his front paw and wave at him. Finn was about to wave back but realized he was holding two boxes of donuts. He smiled instead and turned toward the hallway when Bellow saw him.

"Look at Finn's costume, everyone," Bellow called out.

"I don't see one," said Louis.

"Sure you do," Bellow jeered. "It's him. That's enough to get both screams and laughs from anyone."

Finn thought it would be fun to taunt Bellow about his grim-reaper costume—especially the silly, smiling skeleton mask he wore underneath his black hood. But Finn didn't have time. The parade was about to start, and Botts was waiting for him back in the classroom. He hustled down the hallway to catch up with Tess.

When Tess and Finn returned, the class was in line, ready for the parade.

Finn grabbed the old-man mask and hat off his desk. "Are you sure you want to do this?" he asked, looking at Botts.

"We have the scariest costume in the entire school," Botts replied. "Since we stand taller than anyone else, we scare even the teachers. This is the best day of the year for me. I bet we could even scare the *real* Cornfield Ghost."

Finn pretended not to listen. Whether they could scare the Cornfield Ghost was a question Finn didn't even want to think about.

He hopped onto a chair, jumped on Botts's back, and swung his legs onto Botts's shoulders. Finn pulled the straps of Botts's oversized overalls around his shoulders and fastened them on the front flap. With the overalls fastened, Botts could see only through a small opening. Finn slipped the mask over his head and put the straw hat on. The old-man mask had sunken eyes, a crooked nose, and a screaming mouth.

Ms. Twitchel handed a treat sack to each student. "As we go through each classroom, remember to get a treat from the teacher," she said. "I hear Mr. Spool has huge lollipops you don't want to miss."

Finn hoped the Halloween parade would be as fun as last year's. He needed to get his mind off the Cornfield Ghost. He needed to stop thinking about ways he could embarrass Bellow. He needed a distraction.

CHAPTER THREE

Screams and stares were the reactions of most students watching Ms. Twitchel's class parade through the school.

As they walked out of the last classroom, Finn nudged Botts with his foot. "Botts, you were right. If there had been a scariest-costume award, we would have won. It felt like everyone was screaming at us."

As they followed Ms. Twitchel into the hallway with the rest of the students, Finn saw Bellow teasing Eddy. Bellow, dressed in his grim-reaper costume, was trying to pull

Eddy's underwear out of his soccer shorts but stopped when Ms. Twitchel noticed him.

"Bellow, I'm sure you don't want another detention notice," Ms. Twitchel said. "Please go find the rest of your class." Bellow smirked at Eddy and began pulling his wagon. Inside the wagon was a coffin-shaped box that had been painted black. Finn noticed Bellow's sack of candy inside the box.

Ms. Twitchel turned toward Finn and the rest of the students. "Thanks for staying in line," she said. "Let's go down to the cafeteria. The Halloween carnival is starting. Remember to keep your treat sacks with you. You can use them for the candy you get at the carnival. Follow me."

Botts's shoulders were beginning to ache. "Finn, I think you've gained weight," he said, moaning from inside the overalls. "I'm definitely ready to be a headless ghost."

"Just wait," Finn said, trying to sit still on Botts's shoulders. "We'll be at the lunchroom any moment. I can jump onto a table there."

When Finn and Botts entered the cafeteria, students were everywhere. Oscar was popping orange balloons with darts at one booth, and Cutter was tossing rings onto pumpkins in another. Kids bobbed for apples in big tubs of water, while others tried to eat donuts tied to swinging strings. Outside were a hayride, a maze, and a water-dunking booth with the janitor, Mr. Kleener, as the victim.

In the middle of the cafeteria were open boxes of candy and other treats ready to be handed to students who had tickets.

"Can you hear that?" Botts called out from below Finn's legs.

"What?" Finn responded. "All I can hear is everyone yelling."

"The whole box of red and black licorice ropes is calling for me," Botts said, laughing.

Finn smiled underneath his mask. "You think you're good enough to win an entire box?" Finn asked.

"Did I say anything about winning?" Botts said with a smirk. "I'm buying my candy with a roll of tickets—not by wasting a second trying to win some at a game."

"Tickets are available at the table where Principal Biggs is standing!" Ms. Twitchel shouted to the class. "Have fun today and be safe tonight. Also, don't forget to do your short reading assignment."

Felix turned to Taz. "Who would want to read tonight?" Felix asked defiantly. "I've got better plans—plans to get a whole lot of candy."

Finn overheard Felix. That was exactly the kind of thing a candy thief would say. Felix was definitely someone he needed to keep his eyes on.

After Ms. Twitchel left, Principal Biggs walked over to Finn and Botts. "I make it a point to introduce myself to anyone bigger than me," he said, smiling. "Nice job to both of you. Your costume always scares the entire school."

"Thanks, Principal Biggs," Botts said, his voice muffled by the overalls. "But this old man is just about to get a little shorter."

"OK, OK, I'm jumping down right now," Finn said.

Finn unfastened the overall straps, pulled off the mask and hat, and jumped down onto a table. As Botts rubbed his shoulders, Finn looked outside through the cafeteria windows. He immediately noticed Felix, who was now standing by the dunking booth. After placing someone's treat sack inside his cape,

Felix twirled around in a full circle and then reopened his cape. The sack had disappeared. Felix twirled around again and made the sack reappear. If Felix could make treat sacks disappear with his cape, he could probably use his cape to take treat sacks from unsuspecting students and walk off without anyone knowing. Finn wondered how many treat sacks Felix might have already taken using his cape.

Finn walked over and got in line at the beanbag-toss game, while Botts purchased tickets for both of them. Finn continued to watch Felix as he came inside the cafeteria. He tracked Felix moving toward the apple-bobbing tubs.

Botts interrupted Finn's temporary trance and handed his friend a ticket with a grin. "One for you and a roll for me."

"You really bought a whole roll?" Finn said with a look of surprise on his face. "Once you see my throw, you're not going to need all those tickets."

Within minutes, Finn was standing at the throw line, twelve feet from the front of a large board. The board was covered with pictures of ghosts and bats, spiders and skeletons, and even a few black cats. In the center of the board was a picture of a pumpkin with a wide-open smile. Anyone who threw all three beanbags through the pumpkin's mouth won ten tickets. Finn handed his ticket to a teacher, who placed three black beanbags in his hands. He turned toward Botts and said, "Our sacks will be filled in no time. Trust me—you'll regret buying that roll."

Finn aimed and threw the first beanbag straight into the pumpkin's mouth. The second one followed. But before he could throw the third bag, he heard yelling. It was coming from a princess and a mermaid. They were angry. And Finn knew both of them.

CHAPTER FOUR

Bellow had pushed the heads of Veronica and Deedee into the water tubs while they bobbed for apples. Both were coughing, their faces dripping with water. Bellow was laughing as he walked away.

Finn handed the third beanbag to Botts and dashed over to them. "Are you both OK?" he asked.

"Just a little wet—thanks to Bellow," Deedee grumbled.

She and Veronica looked anxiously around the tubs.

"What's wrong?" Finn asked.

"It looks like someone took our candy sacks," Veronica replied in a teary voice. "They were right next to the tubs when we started— and now they're gone!"

"I'll keep my eyes out for them," Finn said. "And on Bellow, who taped these pieces of paper on your backs." Each read Pinch Me.

Finn turned and watched Bellow continue his teasing crusade. Bellow tied together the capes of two girls dressed as witches and watched them struggle when they walked in opposite directions. He prodded some students at the dart-throwing contest with his scythe, causing them to miss the balloons. He pushed Louis and Victor as they tried to finish the last bite of their dangling donuts in a donut-eating contest. When Bellow walked away, both Louis and Victor had Kick Me signs on their backs.

Finn quickly made his way through the cafeteria crowd and removed the signs.

"Bellow lost it for us," Victor said in an annoyed voice. "And now we can't find our treat sacks."

"Let's go talk to Bellow," Louis hissed. His hands were clenched.

"Hold on," Finn said. "I've been watching Bellow. He's been here the whole time. If he had taken the bags, he would have left and hid them."

"We should at least find the principal and tell him," Victor said.

"I agree," Louis responded.

They both walked toward the doors leading out of the cafeteria.

Finn turned and looked for Felix. Finn spotted Felix outside again, laughing and riding in the hay wagon with some other students. Treat sacks could easily fit not only inside his cape but also under the hay bales.

He looked back at Bellow, who was now walking past Tess. She was doing her best to knock over some bottles labeled with skeleton faces using black rubber balls. As soon as Bellow passed by, Finn saw a Kick Me sign stuck on Tess's back. Finn rushed over and removed it. But this time Bellow noticed.

"So the old man doesn't want to have a little fun?" Bellow shouted. He pushed and shoved his way through a group of students until he was standing face-to-face with Finn.

"You couldn't scare my grandma in your goofy costume," Bellow said, laughing.

"Well . . . there is someone who could scare your grandma," Tess taunted.

"Who'd you have in mind, cow pie?" Bellow sneered, turning to Tess.

"The Cornfield Ghost," Tess replied.

"So you believe in Finn's dumb Cornfield Ghost too?" Bellow teased.

"Sounds like the grim reaper isn't scared of the ghost of old man Grim," Finn said. "Maybe you two should meet. You might be related."

Finn realized he had just thought of the perfect idea. An idea that turned and twisted his stomach.

Tess turned toward Finn. A smile spread across her face. Finn suspected Tess had thought of the same idea but without the turning and twisting.

"Bellow, if you think you're so brave," Tess said confidently, "let's see you walk the cornfield tonight—Friday night. Halloween night."

Finn felt his skin grow cold.

"That's easy," Bellow responded. "But on one condition. You, Finn, and bumble-head Botts agree to give up all your trick-or-treat candy."

"And if you don't walk," Tess replied, "we get yours."

"Deal," said Bellow.

"Be at the field at nine o'clock," Tess said. "Near the baseball diamond."

Finn was in shock.

He would have to go to the cornfield. He would have to hand over his candy to Bellow. And he would have to face his unhappy parents for being out late.

But Bellow wouldn't win.

No one would win.

Because no one would ever walk into the cornfield *tonight*—would they?

Finn feared his worst nightmare was about to come true.

CHAPTER FIVE

For the next two hours, Finn tried to distract himself. He bobbed for apples, won thirty tickets at the beanbag booth, and even searched the hay wagon with Botts for missing candy sacks. But he couldn't stop thinking about meeting Bellow at the cornfield.

Just as Finn began to throw his fourth ball at the dunking-booth lever, which would release the seat underneath a very waterlogged Mr. Kleener, the ten-minute bell rang. School was almost over. Students began to leave the carnival and return to their classrooms.

"Finally," Finn sighed.

Ten minutes later, Principal Biggs started the end-of-school announcements over the intercom.

"I want to thank our teachers and students for making the carnival a success and wish each of you a happy and safe Halloween," Principal Biggs said, pausing. "A number of students have come to me complaining about their missing sacks of candy," he continued in a serious tone. "If you have any information about who took the sacks or where they are, please come to my office immediately. Thanks for your help."

When the final bell rang, Finn, Botts, and Tess hustled outside and down the school steps.

"Who do you think took the candy sacks?" Botts asked.

Finn scratched his head and thought for a moment. "Felix was taking sacks and making them disappear. And some of the kids Bellow was teasing lost their sacks. Both wore a black cape. And last year's candy thief wore a black cape."

They walked in silence until they arrived at Finn's house. Finn thought about the other students he had seen with black capes. Witches, vampires, and even an evil queen. Sylvia also wore a black cape as the circus ringmaster.

"I don't know who did it," Finn blurted in frustration. "But we need to warn the neighborhood. Meet me back here at my house at five o'clock. I have a plan."

Just after 5:00 p.m., Finn walked into the kitchen with a huge stack of flyers and a big bag of dog biscuits. Seated at the table were Tess and Botts, eating pumpkin-shaped cookies that Ms. Fasser had just baked.

"So what's the plan?" Tess asked.

"We need to deliver these flyers and dog biscuits to each house in the neighborhood before kids start to trick or treat," Finn said anxiously.

"Who wants to eat dog biscuits?" Botts said with a disgusted look.

"Read the flyer and you'll know," Finn responded.

Botts read the flyer out loud.

Last year's candy thief may strike again this Halloween.

Many candy sacks were missing at school today.

Please help us stop the thief by placing the dog biscuit inside your trick-or-treat sack.

Writing your name on your sack would help too.

41

Sylvia's dog, Seeker, will be
ready to sniff out the thief!

**REMINDER: DOG BISCUITS
ARE FOR DOGS. DON'T EAT!**

"Finn, if the thief lives in our neighborhood, the thief will know our plan," Tess said
in a worried voice.

"We'll have to take that chance," Finn
replied. "Fortunately, Felix and Bellow live
three blocks away—at least they won't know.
Here's a map of the streets." Finn gave Botts
and Tess each a copy. "I marked on the map
where each of you should go. Be back in one
hour with your costumes."

Tess and Botts each left with a stack of flyers and a small bag filled with dog biscuits.

Finn took the rest and raced out the door
with his map.

Within forty-five minutes, Finn was back home. He grabbed the hat and old-man mask lying on his bed and rushed back downstairs. His dad had already placed his trick-or-treat bag near the front door.

"Something tells me you just might catch your thief tonight," Mr. Fasser said. "You've worked hard."

"Thanks for buying us the dog biscuits," Finn said. "Sylvia's dog can find anybody with those."

"Remember to stay on the sidewalks," Finn's mom added.

Selina overheard them talking and walked into the front hallway. She was wearing white vampire fangs. Her lips were painted blood red.

"I don't know if the old man is capable of staying on any sidewalk," Selina said, smiling. "He can barely see through the mask during the day. I'd be more concerned about him just tripping and falling."

Finn pretended he wasn't listening to her as he watched Botts walk up the sidewalk. He opened the front door.

"Tess is waiting for us at Sylvia's house," Botts said.

"I'm ready," Finn replied.

When they arrived, Tess was standing in the doorway with Sylvia. Seeker was jumping up and down, trying to bite the dog biscuit in Tess's treat sack.

"Thanks for letting us use Seeker," Finn said.

"Seeker will do anything for *those* biscuits," Sylvia replied. "Call or text me if you see or hear anything. We'll be waiting for you right here."

"Thanks," Finn replied. Some small witches and ghosts were walking up the sidewalk. "Ready?" he asked Botts.

Finn climbed onto Botts's shoulders, fastened the overall straps, and put on the mask and hat. Old man Grim was ready to trick or treat.

The sun dimmed as they walked down the sidewalk. Lighted pumpkins carved with ghoulish faces covered the neighborhood's porches and steps. As they went from house to house, Finn imagined some of the glowing pumpkins as secret spies ready to alert the trick-or-treat thief of Finn's presence and others as silent sentinels waiting to assist him in capturing this Halloween bandit.

After one hour, they had rung the doorbell of nearly every house within two blocks. Their trick-or-treat bags were full of candy.

"So much for our thief," Tess sighed. "No black cape. No stolen bags. Nothing."

Finn texted Sylvia on his phone. "Sylvia, no sign of any thief. We're headed back to your house."

Sylvia texted back. "Nothing strange on my end either. See you soon."

"I think it's time to stop worrying about this thief and start worrying about how much candy we want Bellow to get his sticky hands on tonight!" Botts exclaimed. "And if I have to say trick or treat one more time, I'm going to bite my tongue."

Botts continued. "Have either of you even paid attention to what's in your bags? There's a marshmallow mummy from the Wraps, a chocolate coffin from the Naylors, and a caramel-covered apple from the Cores. Of course, the toothbrush we got from Dr. Smiles doesn't excite me too much. But since Tess's dad and Dr. Smiles work together at the same dental office, I won't complain."

As they headed in the direction of Sylvia's house, Finn gazed at the cornfield across the street. It was dark and quiet. He dreaded returning there tonight. He wondered if Bellow would live up to his word.

Suddenly, Finn's phone rang. It was Sylvia. "Come to the Beaders's house quickly!"

CHAPTER SIX

The Beaders lived at the very end of Finn's street.

"We've been waiting all night for this!" Finn shouted. "We can't let the thief get away!"

Finn unfastened the overall straps, pulled his mask off, and jumped down. Botts and Tess followed Finn as all three raced toward the Beaders's. As they approached the streetlight in front of the house, they saw two girls crying, sitting next to Sylvia. Seeker was licking their faces.

"These two girls put their trick-or-treat bags on the lawn to pet the Beaders's cat," explained Sylvia, "and within seconds, someone with a black cape grabbed the bags and ran."

"Did both of you put dog biscuits in your bags?" Finn asked.

Both girls nodded.

"Then you have nothing to worry about," Finn said with confidence. "We'll find the thief and get your treat bags back."

Screaming and yelling interrupted their conversation.

"Sounds like it came from just around the corner!" Tess said.

"Let's go!" Finn shouted.

Finn, Botts, Tess, Sylvia, and Seeker all raced around the corner.

One house down, they found Deedee's younger brother, Scrubby, and his two friends.

They were all sitting on the curb. None of them had their trick-or-treat bags.

"What happened?" Finn asked.

"Someone just took our candy," Scrubby said in despair. "The person just came out of the bushes and pushed us down—and then grabbed all the bags and ran off."

"What was the thief wearing?" Finn asked.

"A black cape," replied Scrubby's friend.

"Which direction did the person go?" Finn said.

"Down that side street across from us," Scrubby said, pointing.

"Did each of you put dog biscuits in your bags?" Finn asked.

All three nodded.

"Great—the more bags our thief steals," Sylvia added, "the more dog biscuits our thief carries. And that means more for Seeker to smell."

"Then our search just got easier," Finn confirmed. He looked over at Scrubby and his friends. "We'll get your bags back."

Finn turned away, wondering if they really could stop this thief. A feeling of panic began to creep over him.

CHAPTER SEVEN

Finn, Botts, Tess, and Sylvia followed Seeker across the street. They searched up and down the side street and adjacent neighborhoods for over thirty minutes. Seeker sniffed just about everything his nose could touch. But he didn't pick up the scent of any dog biscuits.

Finn felt frustrated. "Where's this thief hiding?" he asked.

"That's it," Tess said. "The thief *is* hiding—waiting for us to go away."

"Great time to take a break," Botts said. "This candy looks too good to just haul around all night. Let's go to Sylvia's house. We can hide behind her bushes and trees and wait for the thief to strike again."

"OK," Finn said reluctantly. "Botts, Tess, and I will hide behind the front-porch bushes."

"And Seeker and I will hide behind the big tree next to the street," Sylvia added. "That way Seeker can pick up a scent from anyone walking by."

Sylvia held a dog biscuit in front of Seeker. He barked. "Seeker agrees with your plan," she said with a smile. After Sylvia dropped the biscuit into Seeker's mouth, they all followed Finn back to Sylvia's house.

They walked in silence, looking and listening in all directions, hoping for any sign of the treat-bag bandit.

Finn suddenly stopped. He held out his hands and signaled the others to stay behind him. Just across the street, someone with a long black cape was standing beside three children seated on the bus-stop bench. Whoever it was held three trick-or-treat bags.

"We're not losing the thief this time," Finn whispered to the rest. He turned to the group and then pointed at the bus stop. It was difficult to see clearly with just the glow of the streetlights.

"Do you think that's our thief?" Tess asked, stepping forward.

"We'll soon find out," Finn replied. "Follow me!"

Finn and Tess raced across the street, leaving Botts, Sylvia, and Seeker behind. As they approached, Finn could hear the person wearing the cape talking.

"Your treat bags will now vanish!" the person said. Finn and Tess watched. The thief whirled around and opened his cape.

The treat bags were gone.

"I think we've got our thief," Finn said quietly to Tess. He recognized the flashy voice. He recognized the tall hat on the ground. It could only be Felix.

Felix looked up and noticed Finn and Tess watching him. Finn stopped and watched to see if Felix would run. But he didn't move. Finn turned and looked at each of the three children. They were just smiling and staring at Felix.

"Now I will make them all reappear with a treat inside," Felix announced. He whirled around again, opened his cape, and returned each trick-or-treat bag.

"Wow!" shouted one of the kids after opening his bag. "Look at this red-and-blue sucker I got."

"How did you do that?" asked another.

"A magician never reveals his secrets," Felix replied.

All the children clapped.

"Thank you and have a happy Halloween," Felix responded.

Botts, Sylvia, and Seeker were now standing next to Finn and Tess, watching.

"That's a pretty cool trick," Botts said. He approached Felix. "Here—have my bag."

"Stop," Finn said. "Be serious for a moment. This is no time to be asking for candy from a suspect."

"I am serious," Botts replied.

Felix looked at Finn. "So what's an old man doing out so late?" he said, smiling.

"Someone in a black cape has been stealing candy tonight," Finn said. "Would you happen to know anything about it?"

"I wouldn't call what I do stealing," Felix replied. "Everybody who gives me their bag gets it back—and with one more treat inside."

While Felix and Finn talked, Seeker was sniffing Felix's cape. But Seeker showed no interest in Felix.

Finn smiled sheepishly. "If you happen to see someone with a black cape, let us know," he said.

"You may want to check over at the Hodges's house," Felix suggested. "Someone in a cape and skeleton mask was arguing with a kid."

CHAPTER EIGHT

Finn, Botts, and Tess walked quickly toward the Hodges's house. Sylvia followed closely, pulling on Seeker's leash. Seeker seemed more interested in sniffing every tree, bush, and rock near the sidewalk than trying to find a dog biscuit.

Once they turned the corner onto Finn's street, the Hodges's home was only four houses away. They were now moving so fast they were just short of a sprint. Botts was breathing hard.

"Don't even think about slowing down!" Finn shouted. "We can't let the thief slip away."

When they reached the front yard, a person wearing a black cape and grim-reaper mask was pulling on one end of a candy bag while someone dressed as a witch was pulling on the other.

"Give it to me!" the witch shrieked.

"It's mine," said the hooded figure. "Back off."

Finn raced up and yanked the bag out of the hooded figure's hand.

"What are you trying to do?" a familiar voice yelled.

"We've finally caught you, thief!" Finn said proudly.

"Finn, this is mine," the voice said. The person pulled the hood down and removed the skeleton mask. It was Taz, and the witch was his little sister, Gabby.

"Why are you wearing a grim-reaper costume?" Botts asked.

"The green potion inside my beaker spilled all over my white jacket," Taz explained. "So I had my mom help me make this costume for tonight."

Seeker was barking now, trying to pull Taz's bag out of Finn's hand. The outline of a dog biscuit at the bottom of the bag was clear.

"I see you at least read the flyer," Sylvia said.

"I did," Taz replied. "But I haven't seen anyone stealing anything except for this brat." He poked his sister with his small plastic scythe.

"You agreed," said Gabby, "that if I got more candy than you trick-or-treating, I could pick any two pieces from your bag. So pay up!"

"We'll let you two work things out," Finn said as he handed Taz back his candy.

"We need to start walking over to the cornfield anyway," Tess added.

Finn checked his watch. It was 8:45 p.m.

Tess continued. "Bellow will be there in fifteen minutes. We've got at least a five-minute walk back up the street to the baseball diamond."

Sylvia tugged on Seeker's leash and walked toward her house. "Seeker and I will wait until after nine o'clock to meet you at the cornfield. I don't want Bellow to get suspicious about us."

"Good idea," Finn replied.

Finn, Botts, and Tess quickly crossed the street. A light breeze started to blow. Finn shivered. He wondered if he was shivering because of the cool wind on his skin or the fear of facing the one thing he had warned everyone to stay away from.

CHAPTER NINE

Finn reached the pitching mound and stopped. His watch read 8:52 p.m. The cornstalks, rustling in the breeze, seemed to beckon him. His heart began to beat loudly. Maybe this was how the Cornfield Ghost lured his victims. And once inside, there would be no escape. He closed his eyes to distract himself from the spiraling panic he felt inside.

"Over here," Tess said.

Finn opened his eyes and looked over at the cornfield. Tess had run past him into the field near first base and was now pulling out a black bag hidden in the cornstalks.

"I have everything we need to make sure we don't end up handing over our candy to Bellow," Tess said.

Finn and Botts walked over and watched her pull out a mask and rubber gloves.

Finn looked at Botts in surprise. "You didn't think we were just going to let Bellow walk into the cornfield alone?" Botts added.

"That's exactly what I was thinking," Finn replied.

"Tonight, we take no chances," Tess said. "You and Botts will be the *real* Cornfield Ghost. If Bellow makes it to the well, both of you will be there, ready to give him the scare of his life. Bellow won't recognize you with this mask and rubber gloves."

Tess handed everything to Finn.

Finn looked at the mask in his hands. It was terrifying. It had the face of a demon with pointed ears and fangs. Tess had added red glowing lights to the fiendish eyes, which could be turned on with a small switch on the back of its head. It was something Finn would never want to encounter anywhere. Especially here—on Halloween night.

"Are you crazy?" Finn shouted. "There are no chances to take. Bellow won't even make it past the first five rows before the *real* Cornfield Ghost finds him. Not to mention the fact that the ghost will have already gotten us! Entering the field is nuts."

Before Tess could respond, they heard car tires screeching to a halt. The sound of voices followed. Finn looked at his watch again. It was 8:55 p.m.

They all jumped inside the first row of cornstalks and peered out. Finn could see someone with a long black cape and hood pulling a wagon toward the car. Inside the wagon was a coffin-shaped black box.

"What a haul tonight!" said the person in the cape. They immediately recognized the voice. It was Bellow's.

"That good?" said the voice of the driver. It was Zinnia, who lived near Bellow. She went to high school with Bellow's older sister and had agreed to take Bellow home after he had finished, using Bellow's own words, "the dumbest dare in the world." Bellow had told Zinnia all about his plans for taking candy from trick-or-treaters while she was hanging out at his house with his sister. Zinnia had agreed to act as his accomplice.

"Do you think anyone knows it's you?" asked Zinnia.

Finn, Botts, and Tess watched as Bellow pulled back his hood and removed a white

skeleton mask—the same mask he had worn during the Halloween parade earlier.

"Not the slightest clue," Bellow chuckled. "I've got everything hidden inside my wagon." They both laughed.

"I'll wait for you in the car just past the baseball field," Zinnia replied.

Tess turned to Finn and Botts. "Did you hear that?" she whispered. "You now have even more reason to be in the cornfield tonight. When Bellow sees you coming for him with that demon mask on, he will be so terrified he'll be ready to confess to stealing the trick-or-treat bags."

Finn covered his face with his hands. He felt dizzy. He would have to face his worst nightmare.

Botts looked at Finn. "Even if there is a ghost—you said the ghost is looking for thieves. He won't want us."

"Hurry!" Tess whispered. "It's nine o'clock. Bellow will be coming any second."

Finn moaned. "I can't believe I'm doing this. I can't believe I'm even *thinking* about doing this. Tell my dad and mom I love them. Take care of Tidwell for me. His cat food is in a bin inside the garage."

"You can do this!" Tess said in a low voice.

Finn took a deep breath and looked at the cornfield in front of him. He hoped his heart would stop pounding. He hoped his skin would stop tingling. He hoped the Cornfield Ghost would let him live.

CHAPTER TEN

"Bellow is coming," Tess whispered, pointing toward the street.

"We've got to go now," Botts said, turning to Finn.

Finn stared back. Without waiting for his response, Botts grabbed Finn, pulled him up onto his back, and started running into the cornfield. Botts almost lost his balance as Finn struggled to sit on his shoulders.

"If you could find a place to sit up there sometime soon," Botts said, "you could help

me get to the well. I can't see with all the cornstalks in my face."

Finn didn't respond. He was trying to con-
vince himself he might live if the Cornfield
Ghost got Bellow first.

Minutes went by. Botts continued to push
his way through the tall stalks. The field grew
darker as clouds rolled in, covering the moon.

Finn looked at his watch. 9:05 p.m.

Finn glanced at the Grim house. All the
windows were covered with boards except for
a few in the upstairs rooms. The yard was full
of tall weeds and bushes. A black iron fence
ran along the front and sides of the house,
making it impossible to reach the well any
other way except through the cornfield. Finn
shuddered with fear for a moment as he imagined the Cornfield Ghost suddenly reaching
out from behind the cornstalks with dead-cold
bony hands and a howling, sinister laugh, then

dragging them into the house—the perfect lair for the ghost. Finn hoped his chance of being caught or seen by the ghost was slim. The night sky made it difficult to see anything.

"Start going right a little," Finn said in an uneasy voice. "We're almost near the well at the edge of the backyard. I just don't want to get any closer to the house." Finn had done his best to help guide Botts through the dark field.

"There it is," Finn said, finally spotting the roof of the well right next to the cornfield.

Finn stared at the well as they approached. It was circular and made out of brick, with an old wooden roof held up by two posts. On the underside of the roof was a tarnished bronze bell. This was the same bell he had seen from a distance during the winter months, when the field was empty. He wondered if it was the same bell that had rung long ago on the night old man Grim disappeared. A sick feeling swept over him.

Then something caught his attention. He looked up at the old Grim house. A dim light was on in an upstairs window, and the dark image of someone or something was staring at them.

CHAPTER ELEVEN

"So where are Botts and Finn?" Bellow asked as he approached Tess. "Too scared to show up? Afraid they're going to lose?" He chuckled to himself.

"No reason to worry," Tess replied. "Once you're back, we'll find them, and you can have all our bags."

"You're right," Bellow said. "Let's get started."

Tess continued. "Here's the deal. You have to walk to the well near the old Grim house, ring the bell, and make it back—alive."

"And you probably still think the scary old Cornfield Ghost is going to get me, don't you?" Bellow taunted.

"Let's just say anything is possible," Tess said. "Lulu's dog was never found."

"That's a good thing too," Bellow said, smiling. "That dog was dumb. See you in a minute, cowpoke. And have your bag ready to hand over."

Without another word, Bellow turned on his flashlight and took his first step into the cornfield. He paused for a moment and looked back, then he and his flashlight were gone.

***

By the time he and Botts reached the well, Finn felt like he was going to faint.

"We're dead," Finn whimpered as he pointed to the lighted window. "The Cornfield

Ghost knows we're here. He's been watching us the whole time."

"Snap out of it," Botts said. "It's just a light connected to a timer, shining through a dirty old window. We all know no one lives there. It's designed to trick people into thinking someone's there. And it seems to be working . . . at least on you."

Finn just kept mumbling to himself, "We're gonna die, we're gonna die."

"Stay focused!" Botts snapped. "Bellow may be here any minute. We need to be ready to jump out. We can't let him ring the bell. Do you really want to hand over your candy to him?" At this point, Finn was ready to hand over his treats and everything else he owned if it meant avoiding the ghost of Grim.

Finn nervously fastened the overall clips and pulled on the demon mask and hat. He reached into his pockets and pulled out the rubber gloves. As Finn slipped one glove over each hand, Botts shuffled over to the row of stalks behind the well and hid behind them.

They both were still. Waiting.

The wind continued to rustle the tops of the cornstalks.

Then Finn heard a sound. The sound of footsteps crunching over leaves and weeds.

It was coming from the direction of the house.

He looked toward the house, squinting hard through the slits in the mask. *Strange,* he thought. Why would Bellow be walking toward them from the house? They had all seen Bellow on the south side of the field, where they had left Tess. Finn's heart pounded faster.

Botts tapped Finn's leg. "Look," he whispered. "It's Bellow."

There, moving back and forth toward them through the cornfield, was the beam of a flashlight. Finn could hear Bellow talking to himself, saying, "I can't believe I even agreed to this. Just for three bags. They're probably only half full anyway. I should have asked for more—almost there."

Bellow emerged from the cornstalks. Finn could make out his cape as he walked toward them.

"Well, I'm here," Bellow said to himself. "What a bunch of wimps!" He walked toward the well.

Finn's whole body trembled. Bellow was less than ten feet away. And even worse, Finn was sure the Cornfield Ghost was nearby, ready to snatch all of them.

Botts signaled Finn by grabbing his leg. Finn reached for the switch and turned on the mask's glowing-red eyes. He spread open the cornstalks as Botts stomped into the clearing. Finn thought they would be a terrifying

sight—a red-eyed demon with fangs, towering over the cornstalks.

"Is this some kind of joke?" Bellow shouted. "Is this your new twist on the lame Grim costume? You guys really thought I would fall for—"

Bellow did not complete his sentence.

"WHO DARES ENTER MY CORNFIELD? A THIEF! THIS WILL BE YOUR LAST NIGHT OF STEALING!" said a booming voice.

Bellow screamed, turned, and stumbled, then ran into the cornstalks. The beam of his flashlight, now on the ground, cast an eerie glow on something moving on the path toward them.

Finn and Botts screamed.

Finn pulled off his mask and tried to jump off Botts's shoulders. But he got caught under the overall straps, and the sudden shift in weight caused Botts to lose his balance. They both fell to the ground in shock.

Standing in front of them, holding a pitchfork, was the Cornfield Ghost. It was as real as Finn had imagined.

CHAPTER TWELVE

The ghost moved toward them.

"We didn't mean any harm," Finn pleaded.

The ghost raised his pitchfork.

"Please don't hurt us," Botts begged.

The ghost came closer.

"We were only trying to catch the thief!" Finn cried out. He gasped, closed his eyes for what he thought would be the last time, and waited for the cold, dead hand of the Cornfield Ghost to grab his neck.

"I think I can let you go, then," said the ghost, laughing. "Hi, I'm Tom Grim. It's pretty late for you two to be out in the corn patch. I was sure hopin' to catch that other one. I think he's been stealing candy from kids. I've watched him—with his wagon—come down the street. He's been hiding it in the cornfield and running off, then coming back with bags in his hands. Poor trick-or-treaters. When I saw the cornstalks moving, I thought I should walk out here and find out exactly what was going on."

Finn pushed the overall straps off, stood up, and looked over at Mr. Grim. Finn started to breathe more easily. His heart was no longer pounding. He would see his cat and his family again.

"So you're not a real ghost after all?" Finn asked.

"Nope," Mr. Grim replied. "Sorry to disappoint you. But I thought you two were for a moment. That's not a bad costume. I got a little scared myself when I saw you standing near the well with those red-glowin' eyes."

"So is the story about the ghost of Grim true?" Finn continued.

"I believe my great-grandfather died during the robbery on Halloween night many, many years ago," Mr. Grim said. "No one ever found him. And the thieves escaped. Neighbors have complained to me about something roaming around in this old corn patch and the well bell ringing. But I haven't seen anything since my family began farming this field twenty years ago. So I'll let you decide whether Great-Grandpa's ghost still haunts this field."

Loud barking interrupted their conversation. It was coming from the baseball field, where Finn and Botts had left Tess.

"Sounds like Seeker may have a few answers for us about the missing bags," Finn said.

Mr. Grim and Botts followed Finn back through the cornfield to the baseball diamond. When they emerged, Finn saw Sylvia trying to hold back Seeker. He was barking loudly at something inside the rows of cornstalks closest to the sidewalk.

When Tess saw Mr. Grim, her mouth fell open.

"Don't worry," Mr. Grim said, smiling. "I'm not a ghost. Tom Grim's the name."

"We were both worried when Bellow ran out of the cornfield screaming about a ghost with a pitchfork," Sylvia said. "I was just about to go to Finn's house for help."

"I think the only help we need now," Mr. Grim suggested, "is from your dog."

They all walked toward Seeker, who was whining. His body was halfway inside the first row.

Sylvia and Finn stuck their heads into the cornstalks where Seeker was standing. Just inside was Bellow's wagon, with his coffin-shaped box.

"That is definitely Bellow's wagon," Finn said.

Finn pulled the wagon out of the cornstalks and opened the box flaps. Inside, there were not only bags of candy belonging to trick-or-treaters but also some school candy sacks that belonged to students.

Sylvia and Tess removed all the dog biscuits from the trick-or-treat bags and tossed them to Seeker. The biscuits immediately disappeared into his mouth.

"I think the Cornfield Ghost finally caught his thief," Tess said.

"And I think all future thieves should beware of the ghost," Mr. Grim said with a smile. "So

let's keep the identity of the Cornfield Ghost a secret." Mr. Grim winked.

Finn looked up at the full moon emerging from behind the clouds. The moon seemed to smile back in approval.

"It's getting late," Mr. Grim said. "I'm sure those trick-or-treaters want their candy back."

"And I've got just the plan," Finn replied.

CHAPTER THIRTEEN

With Finn's instructions, Mr. Grim walked back to the house. Fifteen minutes later, he returned driving an old truck. He got out and gave Finn a stack of handwritten notes. Each contained the same message.

"I think these just might do the job," Mr. Grim said.

Finn read one of the notes. "Thanks. They're perfect."

"I also have this," Mr. Grim said, smiling. He pulled out a bright yellow kite from the back of the truck. Torn string hung from its center.

"I found this blown up against the fence last year," he said. "And now that I think about it, I found this exactly one year ago today. I've held on to it, hopin' to find the owner. I thought maybe one of you might know."

"I'm certain it belongs to Jinx," Tess said. "It looks like the yellow kite he lost last Halloween."

"When he sees it, maybe he won't think the Cornfield Ghost is so bad after all," Mr. Grim replied. He looked down at his watch. "It's past 9:45 p.m. We should speed things up a bit. I'm sure your parents are wondering where you are."

Together, they quickly placed the hand-written notes in each of the stolen trick-or-treat bags. Finn attached a note to the kite as well.

"Luckily, every bag has a name on it, so it should be easy to find the right house," said

Finn. He then turned to Tess. "You, Sylvia, and Seeker return the bags to those kids who live on our street. Botts, Mr. Grim, and I will finish the rest."

"Thanks for your help tonight, Mr. Grim," Sylvia said.

"And you tell Seeker thanks for sniffin' out the bags," he replied. "Couldn't have found 'em without his help."

With some assistance from Sylvia, Seeker waved his paw at Finn and Botts as they drove off in Mr. Grim's truck.

After they finished delivering the trick-or-treat bags stolen from neighborhood children and the kite, Mr. Grim drove back to Finn's house. Finn tried to imagine the look of pleasant shock on Jinx's face as he opened his front door tomorrow.

Finn's dad was waiting for them in the doorway as Mr. Grim drove up.

Mr. Grim lifted Bellow's wagon, with the stolen student candy sacks inside, out of the back of the truck and set it down on the sidewalk.

"See ya later, boys," Mr. Grim said, climbing back into the truck.

"Thanks for your help tonight," Finn said as he grabbed the handle of the wagon.

In less than a minute, Mr. Grim was gone, and Botts—with his nonstop yawning—had walked home.

Finn looked at his dad as he pulled the wagon up to the front porch.

"It's a long story," Finn explained. "The short version is I met the Cornfield Ghost tonight and lived."

"I think I want the long version," Mr. Fasser replied. "But it's late. You can tell me in the morning. I want to hear it all."

• • •

The following Monday, Finn's dad dropped him off at school fifteen minutes early. As planned, he was to meet Botts and Tess at the front office. He pulled Bellow's wagon through the front doors of the school and headed toward the principal's office. Tess was standing just outside the main office door.

"What did Flappet say?" Finn asked. Ms. Flappet was Principal Biggs's assistant.

"She was so happy we gave her an apple and a donut last Friday," Tess replied, "that she'll let us leave the wagon in Principal Biggs's office."

"Great!" Finn replied.

Ms. Flappet was talking on the phone as Finn walked in. She managed to wave at Finn as he pulled Bellow's wagon into the principal's office. Finn wasn't sure she recognized him. Her glasses were so thick she usually didn't notice anyone unless they hit the service bell

on the front counter. Botts had been sitting in a chair and immediately got up and followed Finn and Tess.

"Botts, you pull out all the candy sacks and put them on the two chairs in front of Principal Biggs's desk," Finn said.

Finn handed Tess a piece of paper. "Tess, here is a note to tape on Bellow's wagon." Tess read the note.

> The stolen candy sacks were found in this wagon.
>
> The owner of the wagon is Bellow.
>
> You may want to talk to him.

Finn placed one of the handwritten notes from Mr. Grim on the principal's desk.

Ms. Flappet was still on the phone when they walked out of the principal's office. She waved at them again as they walked past her into the school hallway. They now had five minutes to get to class before the bell rang.

As they walked down the hallway, Finn quickly looked inside Ms. Broomfield's classroom. Bellow was not there. One student said he got sick over the weekend from something he saw on Halloween night. Soon the bell rang, and Principal Biggs's voice echoed through the school intercom.

"Good morning, students. I'm happy to announce the stolen candy sacks have been found. I don't know who returned them, but if you're listening, I want to thank you for your help. We think we know who took the sacks. I would also like to read you a note that was on my desk this morning."

Happy Halloween from the Corn-field Ghost!

PS: Beware, thieves! The Cornfield Ghost is watching.

Principal Biggs paused. "I don't know who this ghost is. But if any of you do, please tell him we hope he's available to help next year."

Finn grinned. The thief had been caught, the candy sacks had been found, and a ghost had become his friend. Not a bad result for one night's work. And that didn't include all the extra candy from Bellow's sack that was just waiting at home for him to eat.

ABOUT THE AUTHOR

Stew Knight is the author of the Finn & Botts chapter book series. Despite being one of the most avid readers and attentive students in his second-grade class, he would still find it funny to yell at random moments to disrupt his teacher if she was being too boring—a stunt that his teacher didn't let slide without discipline. But the discipline worked, because Knight's imagination developed to the point where nothing was ever boring again. He thanks his second-grade teacher for helping his imagination grow enough to become an author.

Knight lives in Salt Lake City, Utah, with his wife and very anxious poodle. He enjoys the outdoors and can be found on the ski slopes in the winter, hiking the Wasatch Range of the Rocky Mountains in the spring and summer, and hanging out with the pigs at the annual state fair in the fall.

DISCARD

CPSIA information can be obtained
at www.ICGtesting.com
Printed in the USA
LVHW111417251020
669761LV00004B/1041